# THE WONDROUS DINOSAURIUM

Written by
## John Condon

For Eddie and Alex - JC

Illustrated by
## Steve Brown

For Alison, Harry, Megan and Carmela
for all your love and support - SB

Danny's mum finally agreed that he could have a pet.
But he didn't want a puppy, a kitten, or even a parrot.

No, he wanted something exciting, something prehistoric, something like...

...a **DINOSAUR!**

And he knew **exactly** where to find one. Although the shop **looked** small on the outside, inside there was...

... EVERY... DINOSAUR ... EVER.

"**Welcome**," said a loud man in an even louder suit.

"I'm Mr Ree, purveyor of prehistoric pets. Please, take your *pick!*"

Danny pointed at the first dinosaur to catch his eye.
"I want **THAT** one," he said.

"Ahaa," replied Mr Ree. "**Diplodocus Longus**, from the Late Jurassic period. It requires half a ton of vegetation per day."

Danny was happy with his choice, **but...**

...he **soon** changed his mind.

"Have you got one that's less **massive?**" asked Danny.

"But of course," replied Mr Ree. "I have smaller ones, slimmer ones, flatter ones and thinner ones. The choice is yours."

Danny pointed into the shadows. "I'll take **THAT** one," he said.

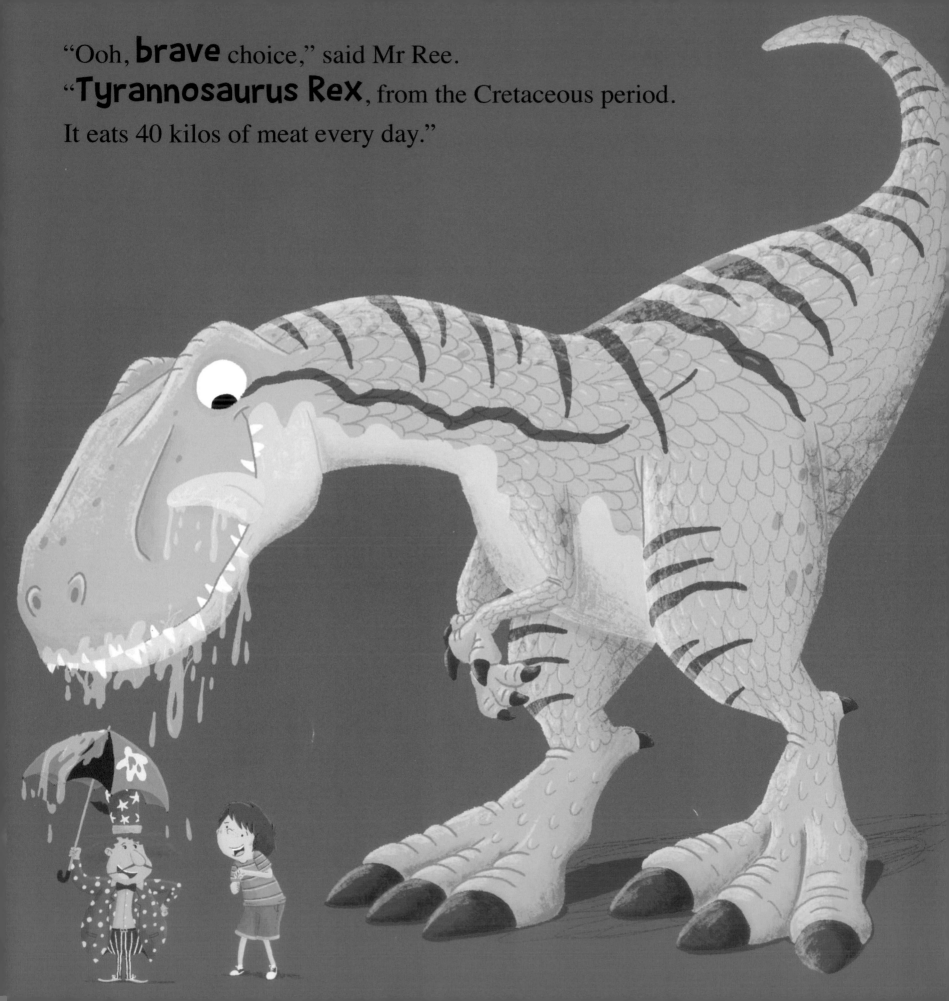

"Ooh, **brave** choice," said Mr Ree.
"**Tyrannosaurus Rex**, from the Cretaceous period.
It eats 40 kilos of meat every day."

Danny **quickly** changed his mind again.

"Have you got one that's less **drooly?**" he asked.

"Indeed I have," replied Mr Ree. "I have chewy ones, slurpy ones, licky ones and burpy ones. Whatever takes your fancy."

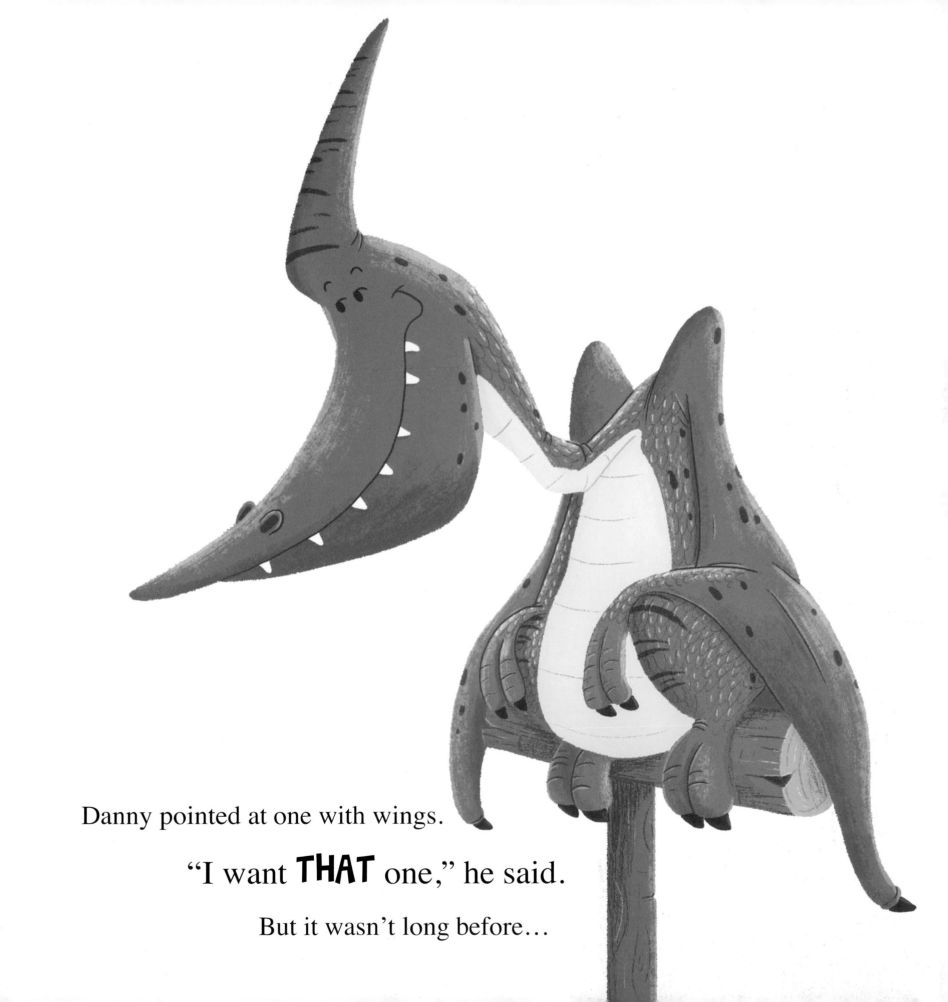

Danny pointed at one with wings.

"I want **THAT** one," he said.

But it wasn't long before…

"I've changed my

Danny tried other dinosaurs as well...

"THAT one!"

"THAT one!"

Aaa-choo!

"THAT one!"

"THAT one!"

...but none of them were **quite** right.

"What next?" asked Mr Ree. "I have swirly ones and spotty ones, stripy ones and dotty ones. **SO** many more to choose from."

But Danny didn't **want** to choose another one.
Until, that is, he saw something in the darkest corner of the shop.

"Wait," he said, "**THIS** one is **perfect.**"

Danny took his new pet home
to show his mum.

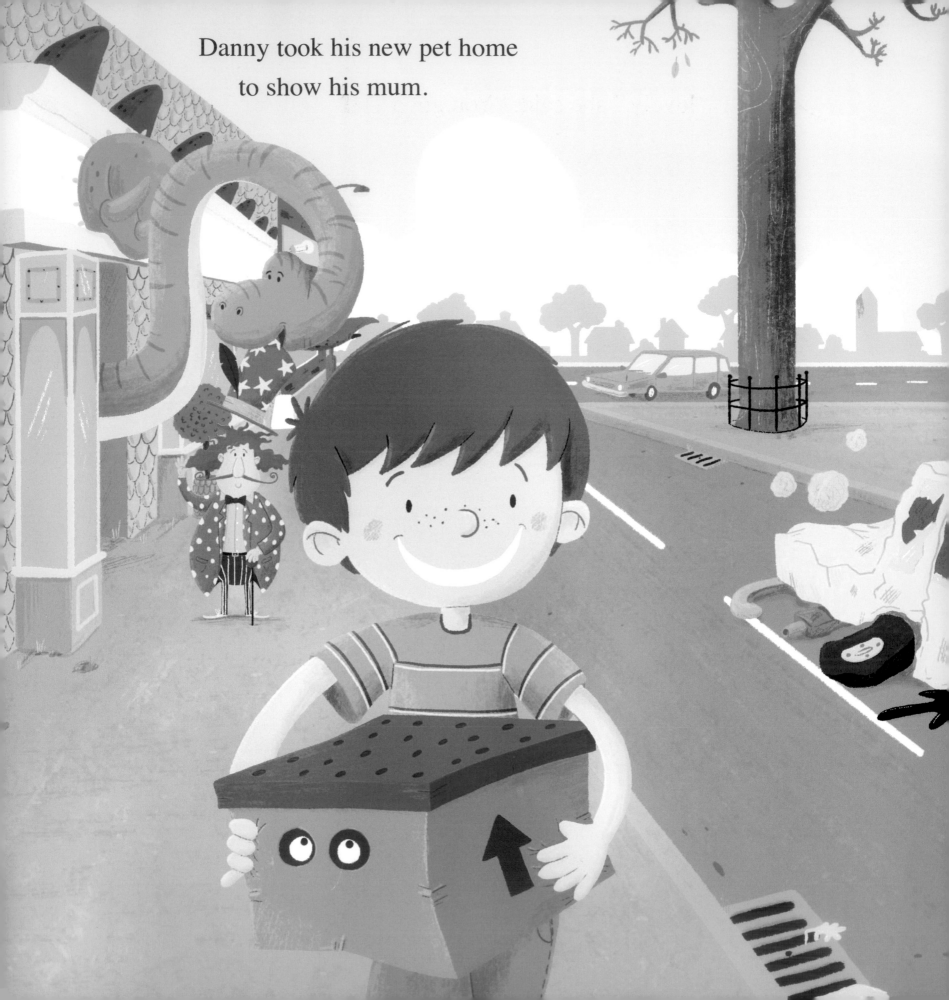

"How lovely," she said. "You got a **tortoise**."

"I did **not** get a boring tortoise," replied Danny.

## "I got a **DINOSAUR!**"

Meiolania:
Middle Miocene Epoch

**The Wondrous Dinosaurium**
An original concept by author John Condon
© John Condon
Illustrated by Steve Brown

MAVERICK ARTS PUBLISHING LTD
Studio 3A, City Business Centre, 6 Brighton Road, Horsham, West Sussex, RH13 5BB
© Maverick Arts Publishing Limited   +44 (0)1403 256941

Published May 2018

A CIP catalogue record for this book is
available at the British Library.

ISBN 978-1-84886-323-1

Maverick
arts publishing
www.maverickbooks.co.uk